PRO FOOTBALL'S CHAMPIONSHIP

BY TYLER OMOTH

CAPSTONE PRESS
a capstone imprint

Blazers Books are published by Capstone Press,
1710 Roe Crest Drive, North Mankato, Minnesota 56003
www.mycapstone.com

Copyright © 2018 by Capstone Press, a Capstone imprint. All rights reserved.
No part of this publication may be reproduced in whole or in part, or stored in a
retrieval system, or transmitted in any form or by any means, electronic, mechanical,
photocopying, recording, or otherwise, without written permission of the publisher.

Library of Congress Cataloging-in-Publication Data
Names: Omoth, Tyler, author.
Title: Pro football's championship / by Tyler Omoth.
Description: North Mankato, Minnesota : An imprint of Capstone Press, [2018]
   | Series: Major Sports Championships | Series: Blazers | Audience: Ages:
   8-14.
Identifiers: LCCN 2017028546 (print) | LCCN 2017032210 (ebook) | ISBN
   9781543504477 (eBook PDF) | ISBN 9781543504798 (hardcover)
Subjects: LCSH: Super Bowl—History—Juvenile literature. | National Football
   League Championship Game—Juvenile literature. | Football—United
   States—History—Juvenile literature.
Classification: LCC GV956.2.S8 (ebook) | LCC GV956.2.S8 O43 2018 (print) |
   DDC 796.332/64—dc23
LC record available at https://lccn.loc.gov/2017028546

Editorial Credits
Carrie Braulick Sheely, editor; Kyle Grenz, designer; Eric Gohl, media researcher;
Kathy McColley, production specialist

Photo Credits
Dreamstime: Jerry Coli, 20, 23, Mbr Images, 21, Wojciech Kimborowicz, 22; Getty
Images: Focus On Sport, 7, 11, Sylvia Allen, 16; Newscom: Fotosports International,
19, Icon SMI/TSN, 14, Icon Sports Media, 15, MCT/Harry E. Walker, 12, MCT/
Mark Cornelison, 28, Sipa USA/Anthony Behar, 4–5, SportsChrome/Tony Tomsic, 8,
UPI Photo Service/Bruce Gordon, 26–27, USA Today Sports/Robert Deutsch, cover,
ZUMA Press, 25

Design Elements: Shutterstock

Printed and bound in the USA.
010754S18

TABLE OF CONTENTS

AN AMAZING COMEBACK........4
**HISTORY OF
THE SUPER BOWL.............6**
GREATEST DYNASTIES.........14
ASTOUNDING SUPER BOWLS....24

GLOSSARY 30
READ MORE 31
INTERNET SITES................31
INDEX........................32

AN AMAZING COMEBACK

Late in the 2017 Super Bowl, the Patriots trailed the Falcons by 25 points. Then Patriots' quarterback Tom Brady threw pass after pass until the game was tied. The Patriots topped it off with a **touchdown** for the win.

touchdown—when the ball is carried or caught past the goal line in football, scoring 6 points

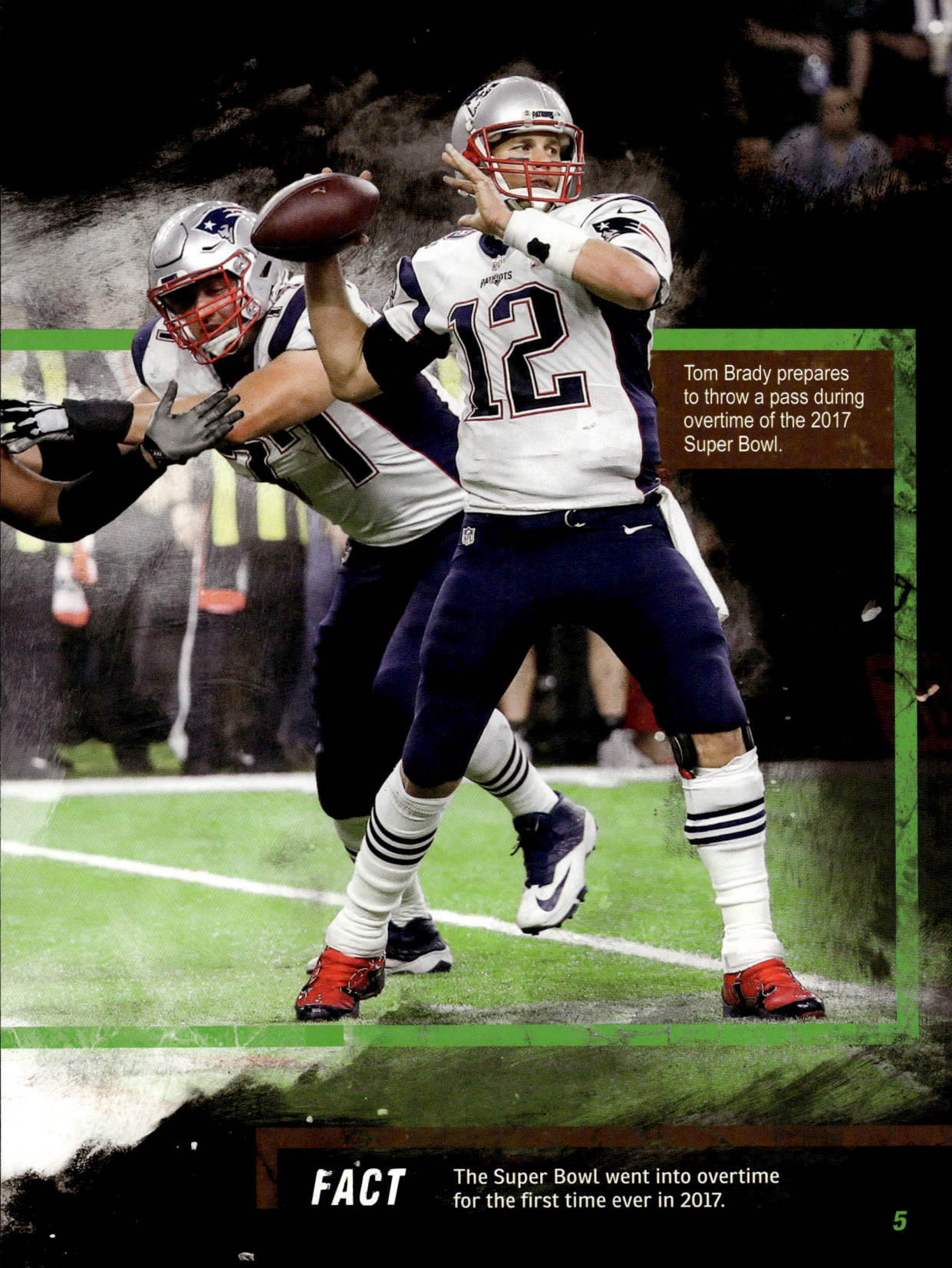

Tom Brady prepares to throw a pass during overtime of the 2017 Super Bowl.

FACT The Super Bowl went into overtime for the first time ever in 2017.

HISTORY OF THE SUPER BOWL

The history of the Super Bowl goes back to the 1960s. Two pro football leagues were in action. These were the National Football League (NFL) and the American Football League (AFL). The leagues did not play against each other.

FACT In 2017 more than 170 million fans tuned in to watch Super Bowl LI. It was the most watched program in the history of American television.

The New York Jets face off against the Buffalo Bills in a 1966 AFL game.

The NFL and AFL agreed to play a championship game. Each league's best team faced off in 1967. They called it the AFL-NFL World Championship. The NFL's Green Bay Packers beat the AFL's Kansas City Chiefs 35-10.

FACT The 1967 and 1968 AFL-NFL World Championship games are now known as Super Bowl I and Super Bowl II.

Packers' quarterback Bart Starr drops back to fire a pass in the 1967 AFL-NFL World Championship game. He was named the game's Most Valuable Player (MVP).

In 1969 the championship game was renamed the Super Bowl. In 1970 the two leagues formed the new NFL. It had two **conferences** called the National Football Conference (NFC) and the American Football Conference (AFC). Each conference put teams in four **divisions**.

FACT Kansas City Chiefs owner Lamar Hunt named the Super Bowl. The name came from the bouncy balls his children played with called Super Balls.

conference—a group of athletic teams

division—a small group of teams in a conference that compete against one another; divisions are often grouped by location

Ralph Baker of the New York Jets pushes to gain yards against the Baltimore Colts in the 1969 Super Bowl.

FACT A different U.S. city hosts the Super Bowl each year. The NFL chooses the city three to five years in advance.

In 2009 the Pittsburgh Steelers earned their sixth Super Bowl title after defeating the Arizona Cardinals.

Each season six teams from each conference go to the playoffs. These teams are the four division champions and two **wild card** teams. After three rounds of playoff games, each conference has a champion. These two teams face off in the Super Bowl.

MOST TEAM SUPER BOWL WINS

TEAM	WINS
PITTSBURGH STEELERS	6
SAN FRANCISCO 49ERS	5
DALLAS COWBOYS	5
NEW ENGLAND PATRIOTS	5

wild card—a team that advances to the playoffs without winning its division; wild card teams advance to the playoffs based on their conference regular-season record

GREATEST DYNASTIES

Some teams win so much that they build a **dynasty**. The Green Bay Packers won three NFL championships in the early 1960s. But that was just the start. They also won Super Bowls I and II.

Quarterback Bart Starr led his team to its 1966 championship win against the Cleveland Browns.

FACT The winner of the Super Bowl receives the Vince Lombardi Trophy. The trophy is named for Packers head coach Vince Lombardi. He led the Packers to their first Super Bowl win.

dynasty—a team that wins multiple championships over a period of several years

Steelers' star running back Franco Harris plows ahead during the 1975 Super Bowl against the Minnesota Vikings.

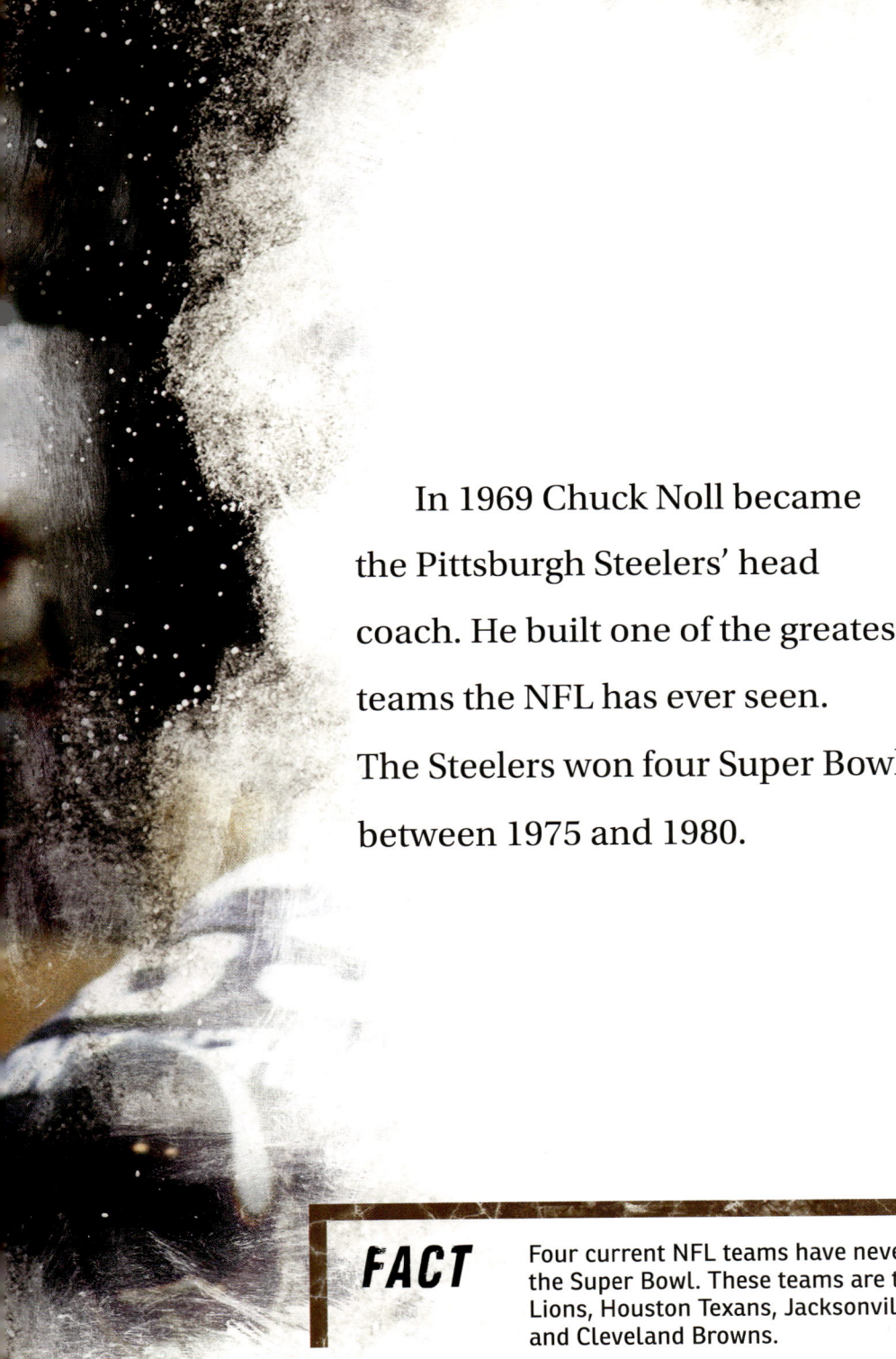

In 1969 Chuck Noll became the Pittsburgh Steelers' head coach. He built one of the greatest teams the NFL has ever seen. The Steelers won four Super Bowls between 1975 and 1980.

FACT Four current NFL teams have never reached the Super Bowl. These teams are the Detroit Lions, Houston Texans, Jacksonville Jaguars, and Cleveland Browns.

From 1981 to 1990, the San Francisco 49ers won four Super Bowls. Head Coach Bill Walsh had a great **offense**. Wide receiver Jerry Rice sliced through **defenses**. Quarterback Joe Montana zipped passes into his receivers' hands.

MOST CAREER SUPER BOWL TOUCHDOWNS

PLAYER	TEAM	TOUCHDOWNS
JERRY RICE	SAN FRANCISCO 49ERS	8
EMMITT SMITH	DALLAS COWBOYS	5
THURMAN THOMAS	BUFFALO BILLS	4
JOHN ELWAY	DENVER BRONCOS	4
FRANCO HARRIS	PITTSBURGH STEELERS	4
ROGER CRAIG	SAN FRANCISCO 49ERS	4

offense—team members who are trying to score points

defense—team members who are trying to stop points from being scored

Jerry Rice played for the San Francisco 49ers for 15 seasons.

Troy Aikman was named the winningest quarterback of any decade for his performance in the 1990s. He had 90 wins in the 10-year span.

The 1989 season was tough on the Dallas Cowboys. The team had just one win. The Cowboys needed star players. They got them in quarterback Troy Aikman and running back Emmitt Smith. Dallas won three Super Bowl titles from 1993 to 1996.

Emmitt Smith became the NFL's all-time leading rusher.

Head coach Bill Belichick and quarterback Tom Brady joined the New England Patriots in 2000. The mix turned into magic. The Patriots won three Super Bowls from 2002 to 2005. Years later, Brady led the team to Super Bowl wins in 2015 and 2017.

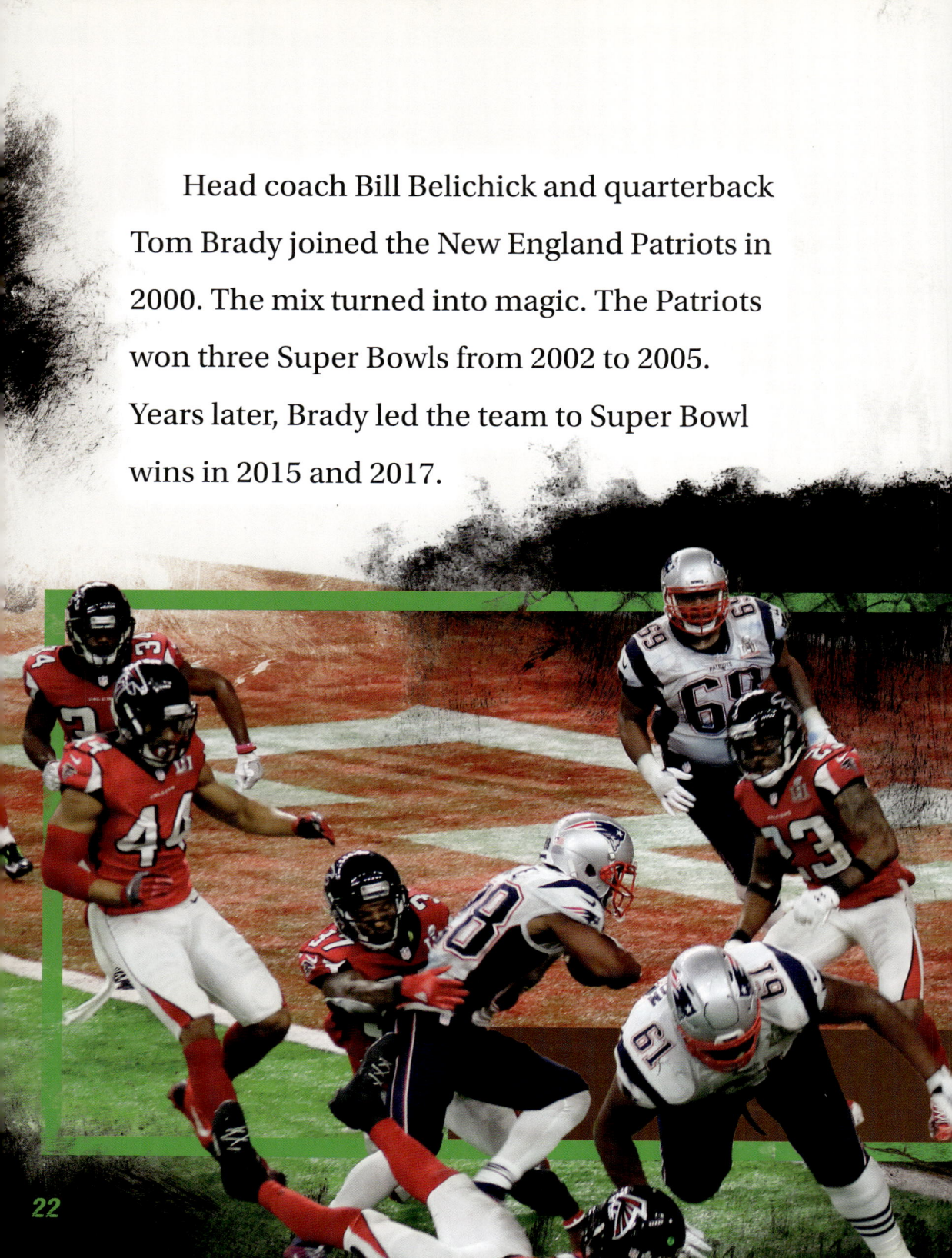

MOST SUPER BOWL MOST VALUABLE PLAYER (MVP) AWARDS

PLAYER	POSITION	TEAM	MVPS
TOM BRADY	QUARTERBACK	NEW ENGLAND PATRIOTS	4
JOE MONTANA	QUARTERBACK	SAN FRANCISCO 49ERS	3
TERRY BRADSHAW	QUARTERBACK	PITTSBURGH STEELERS	2
ELI MANNING	QUARTERBACK	NEW YORK GIANTS	2
BART STARR	QUARTERBACK	GREEN BAY PACKERS	2

The Patriots score their winning touchdown in the 2017 Super Bowl.

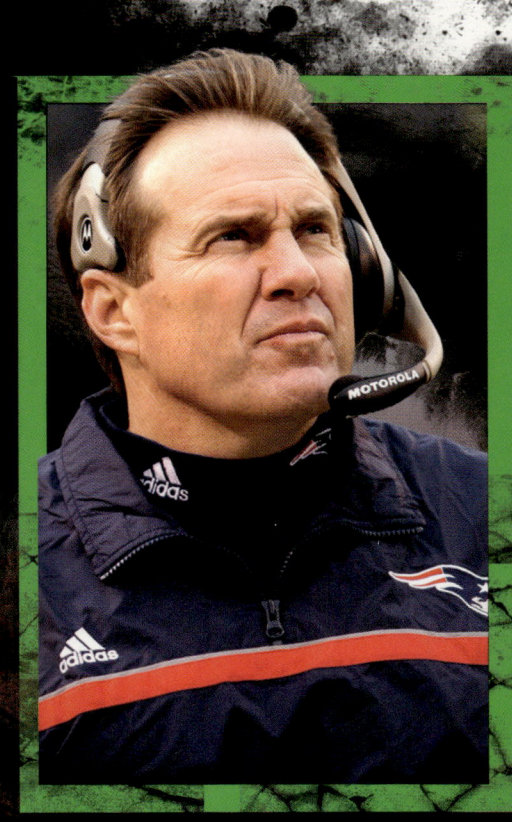

FACT

In 2016 Belichick passed Chuck Noll's record for the most Super Bowl wins by a head coach.

ASTOUNDING SUPER BOWLS

All Super Bowls are exciting, but some are thrillers. In 2009 the Steelers trailed the Cardinals. Steelers' quarterback Ben Roethlisberger zipped the ball to the **end zone**. Santonio Holmes stretched for the catch. Touchdown! The Steelers won.

FACT In 1990 the San Francisco 49ers scored 55 points to beat the Denver Broncos in Super Bowl XXIV. They broke a Super Bowl record for the highest-scoring winners.

end zone—the area between the goal line and the end line at either end of a football field

Santonio Holmes' feet barely scraped the grass during his touchdown catch in the 2009 Super Bowl.

FACT In 1980, 103,985 fans crowded into the stadium to watch the Steelers play the Rams in Super Bowl XIV. It set a record for the biggest Super Bowl crowd.

Kevin Dyson stretches for the end zone in a last effort to win Super Bowl XXXIV.

In 2000 the St. Louis Rams had a 7-point lead. Tennessee Titans' quarterback Steve McNair threw the ball to Kevin Dyson. Dyson raced for the end zone as the clock ran out. But Rams' linebacker Mike Jones wrapped up Dyson's legs. Dyson fell just inches from the end zone. The Rams won.

The Patriots had a 14-10 lead at the end of the 2007 Super Bowl. Giants' quarterback Eli Manning threw to David Tyree. Tyree jumped up and pinned the ball against his helmet. The pass was complete! The Giants **upset** the Patriots 17-14.

FACT For Super Bowl LI in 2016, the average cost for a ticket was $5,216. At Super Bowl I, the highest price was $12.

Rodney Harrison fought hard for the ball, but Tyree kept it pinned against his helmet.

upset—to defeat unexpectedly

Glossary

conference (KON-fur-uhnss)—a group of athletic teams

defense (dee-FENS)—team members who are trying to stop points from being scored

division (di-VIZH-uhn)—a small group of teams in a conference that compete against one another; divisions are often grouped by location

dynasty (DYE-nuh-stee)—a team that wins multiple championships over a period of several years

end zone (END ZOHN)—the area between the goal line and the end line at either end of a football field

offense (aw-FENSS)—team members who are trying to score points

touchdown (TUHCH-down)—when the ball is carried or caught past the goal line in football, scoring 6 points

upset (up-SET)—to defeat unexpectedly

wild card (WILD CARD)—a team that advances to the playoffs without winning its division

Read More

Blaine, Richard. *Cups, Bowls, and Other Football Championships.* Football Source. New York: Crabtree, 2016.

Braun, Eric. *Super Bowl Records.* Everything Super Bowl. North Mankato, Minn.: Capstone, 2017.

Storden, Thom. *Amazing Football Records.* Epic Sports Records. North Mankato, Minn.: Capstone, 2015.

Internet Sites

Use FactHound to find Internet sites related to this book.

Visit *www.facthound.com*

Just type in **9781543504798** and go.

Check out projects, games and lots more at
www.capstonekids.com

Index

AFL-NFL World
 Championship, 9
Aikman, Troy, 21
American Football
 Conference (AFC), 10

Belichick, Bill, 22, 23
Brady, Tom, 4, 22

Dallas Cowboys, 21
Dyson, Kevin, 27

Green Bay Packers, 9, 14

Holmes, Santonio, 24
Hunt, Lamar, 10

Manning, Eli, 29
Montana, Joe, 18

National Football
 Conference (NFC), 10
New England Patriots, 4, 22, 29
Noll, Chuck, 17, 23

Pittsburgh Steelers, 17, 24, 26
playoffs, 13

Rice, Jerry, 18

San Francisco 49ers, 18, 24
Smith, Emmitt, 21

Tyree, David, 29

Vince Lombardi Trophy, 14